MOVING THE GOALPOSTS

This edition published 2010
First published 1998 by
A & C Black Publishers Ltd
36 Soho Square, London, W1D 3QY

www.acblack.com

Text copyright © 1998 Rob Childs
Illustrations copyright © 1998 Gary Rees
Cover illustration copyright © 2010 Maya Gavin

The rights of Rob Childs and Gary Rees to be
identified as author and illustrator of this work respectively
have been asserted by them in accordance with the
Copyrights, Designs and Patents Act 1988.

ISBN 978-1-4081-2234-1

A CIP catalogue for this book is available
from the British Library.

This book is produced using paper that is made from wood
grown in managed, sustainable forests. It is natural, renewable and
recyclable. The logging and manufacturing processes conform to
the environmental regulations of the country of origin.

Printed and bound in China by C&C Offset Printing.

MOVING THE GOALPOSTS

Rob Childs

Illustrated by Gary Rees

A & C Black • London

PENALTY!

Sam crouched on the goal-line, feeling as if the whole world was watching him. He fidgeted with his gloves, knocking the mud off them, and bounced up and down on his toes.

Good luck, keeper!

It's all up to you, Sam.

He glanced around at his team-mates. They were strung along the edge of the penalty area like a row of yellow shirts on a washing line.

Sam knew the score all right. They didn't have to tell him that. But Daniel, the team captain, wanted Sam to be aware of something else.

The penalty-taker smiled. He decided to play a game of double-bluff, hoping the keeper would think he'd aim to the right.

On the referee's whistle, the boy loped forwards and did a little jink run-up to try and confuse the keeper even more. His body disguised the direction of the kick well, but Sam saw the flicker of the eyes that gave him away.

As he struck the ball to the left, Sam dived.

Great stop!

Magic, Sam! Saved us again.

SMACK

Sam scrambled to his feet, grinning hugely and hugging the ball to his chest. Southfield School's Year 7 football team mobbed their goalie in delight.

C'mon, team. Sam's kept us in the game. Let's grab that equaliser now.

Sam booted the ball away upfield, but it soon came back into his own half. The home team were proving too strong. They had dominated the match right from their first attack.

On the touchline, Southfield's sports teacher, Mr Rogers, shook his head.

But even Sam couldn't prevent a second goal for ever. Ten minutes from the end, a tall striker leapt, unchallenged, for a corner and headed the ball firmly past the helpless keeper.

Ajit, Southfield's leading scorer, was not impressed by the teacher's demands.

There was no further scoring until the final minute of the game. The goal went to Southfield, but it only proved a consolation effort. A rare lapse by his marker allowed Ajit a clear view of the target and he tucked his shot neatly into the net.

Southfield trooped off the pitch, heads down.

Oh, well. 2-1. Could have been worse, I suppose.

It was soon to become much worse for Sam. As they changed in the cloakroom, Mr Rogers called out above the noise.

It was an honour they all dreaded. His team-mates cheered with relief that the teacher hadn't picked on them this time. Mr Rogers seemed to enjoy watching someone squirm in front of a smirking Year Group assembly, especially if the player had to explain how a match was lost.

Sam didn't hear the comments. His senses had been numbed. Leering faces swam before his eyes, the sound distorted. All the pleasure and excitement of his performance had suddenly vanished. A sense of panic washed over him instead and sweat broke out on his forehead.

In desperation, still half-dressed, he went up to the teacher to try and have a word in private.

Sam hoped nobody would overhear what he said, but the teacher's reply was agonisingly loud.

Sam glanced round nervously, knowing that his team-mates were listening.

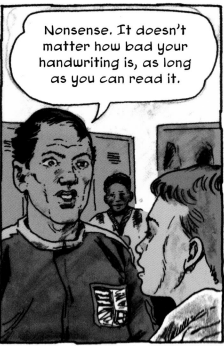

Sam shuffled his bare feet.

'No excuses,' said the teacher, losing his patience.

Sam was the last one to leave the changing room, unable to find his socks. He was past caring. He stuck his feet into his cold trainers and slouched into the car park.

Daniel's parents were waiting to drive him home. He climbed into the car without speaking, his face sickly white.

What's up? Is it having to write that report?

Sam nodded. The very thought of it made his stomach churn.

Sam smiled weakly, trying to hide his fears. He hadn't told his mates the real reason why he'd got on the wrong bus that day after the match.

The truth was that he'd read the number back to front, mistaking 12 for 21.

For Sam didn't always see things quite like other people. He tended to jumble up numbers, and his letters, too, without realising. Until recently, he hadn't understood why his reading and spelling were so poor, but now he knew.

After he'd attempted a series of tests, an educational psychologist had explained to his parents what was different about him. He was dyslexic.

OUT OF ACTION

Sam was away from school until Thursday. On his return, he was greeted in the classroom by Ajit, who seemed to delight in telling him the bad news.

Sam shrugged and gave him a quick grin.

Mrs Brown, their form teacher, came into the room.

Pleased to see you back, Sam – and I know somebody else who will be as well.

Who's that, Miss?

Mr Rogers. He wants you to go to the changing rooms straight after registration. I'm not sure what it's about.

A few sniggers were heard around the room. Everyone else knew.

Daniel and Josh, the team's centre-back, caught up with a miserable-looking Sam at morning break.

I've been banned.

Banned! You're joking!

No joke. Rogers has dropped me from next Saturday's league game. He said I don't deserve to play, just 'cos I went and missed that stupid assembly.

The captain was horrified.

But we need you. No one else is any good in goal.

Dad will go beserk when he hears. He knows what was making me ill.

The thought of having to write that report, you mean?

Sam nodded.

He's already planning to come in and have a word with Mrs Brown about things.

25

Sam felt his fists clench. Josh often came out with snide remarks when he saw Sam struggling to do something in class.

Sam moved menacingly towards Josh, making him back-pedal.

Disconnected, am I? Right – maybe I'll disconnect you now, bit by bit! See how you like it.

Josh quickly made himself scarce.

Ignore him, Sam, you know what he's like. Let's go and join in the kickabout on the field.

Sam's mood improved when he felt a football in his hands again.

He took his frustration out on the ball by hoofing it powerfully away at any opportunity.

First, he pretended it was Josh's head, then Mr Rogers', and by the bell he felt more like his old self again.

By Saturday morning, though, Sam still hadn't got over the disappointment of having to miss the match. He turned up to watch instead and could hardly believe his eyes. Their wooden goalposts were lying on the pitch, broken into pieces. The footballers stared at the wreckage in dismay.

Sam pulled a face.

Neither could the reserve goalkeeper. The very first shot of the game soared over his head out of reach – but still passed underneath the high bar into the goal. So did another soon afterwards. The reserve's confidence was shattered and he even ended up letting two goals in through his legs.

How Sam wished he could have been playing. The team might still have lost, but perhaps not so heavily. The final score was 8-2 and Sam felt he had somehow let everyone down.

The team's next football practice on Tuesday afternoon took place in the big goals, too. Ajit loved it. Within minutes he chipped the ball into the far top corner, well behind Sam's flailing arms.

The goalkeeper was not amused.

What a goal! Easy! Easy!

I don't stand a chance in these things. That would have gone miles over the bar normally.

Sam hated letting in goals at the best of times. He couldn't bear the thought of being beaten by unstoppable shots in all their future home games. When he complained, Mr Rogers merely responded with a shrug.

The following day, after school, Sam's father came to speak to Mrs Brown. He was dyslexic himself and understood the kind of difficulties his son was facing in lessons.

Sam sat in the classroom with them, but he was only half listening to the conversation. It seemed there wasn't enough money to pay for a specialist teacher to give him the extra help he needed to cope with his work.

But Sam's been officially diagnosed now as dyslexic. I want to know what the school's going to do about it.

Sam's interest suddenly perked up when he heard that.

As his dad continued to discuss the situation with Mrs Brown, Sam turned the new phrase over in his mind.

Suddenly, he was struck by a brilliant idea.

Right! If other people can go and move the goalposts, then so can I!

DESIGNER GOALS

Sam was busy that evening. The dining table was covered with paper and the waste bin by his chair was full of crumpled sheets.

40

Sam wanted to check that the spelling was correct before he showed the plans to Mr Rogers. His mum helped him with that.

The only words he was sure about were those of his own name. He'd learnt them off by heart years ago, but he didn't always notice if his 'N's and 'S's were the right way round. He scrawled the title across the top in capital letters.

Sam worked with his dad all weekend, measuring, cutting and drilling the long tubes of metal. They welded some of the sections together, but others were fixed by bolts so that they could be taken apart.

At Sunday teatime, Sam gave Mum a progress report.

Sam made a point of speaking to the sports teacher first thing on Monday morning.

Me and my dad are making these vandal-proof metal goals for the school, Mr Rogers.

Great. How big are they?

45

Sam returned to the team on Wednesday for a friendly fixture that they won 4–1, thanks to a hat-trick from Ajit.

But as they changed afterwards, the boys knew that Saturday's cup tie against Brimthorpe would be much tougher.

I'm dying to see these home-made wonder goals of yours, Sam. Make sure you get them the right way up! The crossbar goes at the top, remember!

47

The goals were ready in time – but only just. Sam spent Friday evening giving them their final coat of white paint, his head still reeling from the exciting news he'd heard that day. The school had at last received an extra grant of money to use for the benefit of all their dyslexic pupils.

About time, too. The individual teaching will be a tremendous help in improving your reading and writing abilities, Sam. And I'm sure you'll make the most of it.

Next morning, when the players arrived at school for the match, they found Sam and his dad still setting up the goals on the pitch.

Leaving it a bit late, aren't you?

Sam wound up the long tape measure and grinned.

Just a few last-minute technical hitches. Had a spot of bother getting the goals in the back of our van. But everything's OK now – I think.

They're magic, Sam. Much better than using those big 'uns.

Yeah, best own goal I've ever seen!

Huh! Not even any nets on them.

Sam heard Josh's loud sneer but let the remark pass. None of the school's goals had nets, either.

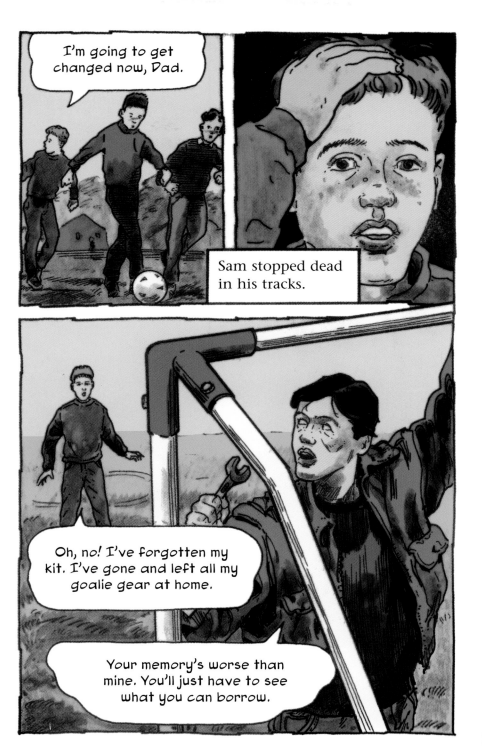

Ten minutes later, Sam trooped out of the changing room feeling strange and nervous. Strange because of his baggy top, odd socks and tight boots. Nervous because he so much wanted his goals to be a success.

At least Mr Rogers had told him they seemed fine, even though the teacher hadn't had the chance to inspect them close-up yet.

It didn't take long for the new goals to be christened.

Unfortunately, the dubious honour of being the first keeper to concede a goal in them fell to their maker. Sam lay on the wet ground, well beaten by a deflected, skidding drive.

As Sam picked himself up, he was in for a surprise. Josh actually apologised.

Bit cruel, that deflection. Soz! I tried to block the shot.

Not your fault. Just forget it and get on with the game.

With the wind in their favour, Southfield hit back strongly and forced Brimthorpe onto the defensive.

The glistening posts soon sported their first dirty mark as a volley from Ajit clanged against one of the metal uprights.

A swift counter-attack from the visitors, however, almost put Southfield further behind.

Always on the alert, Sam dived full-length to pull off an acrobatic save, turning the ball around a post for a corner.

This swung across into the goalmouth and a furious scramble was ended by the ball being blasted just over the crossbar.

That comment from Josh was music to Sam's ears. It made every minute spent working on the goals seem worthwhile.

It was the captain himself who finally levelled the scores.

Daniel went on a solo run towards goal, jinking his way through two tackles before sliding the ball under the keeper's body.

C'mon. Let's really get stuck into 'em now!

SAME FOR BOTH SIDES?

Brimthorpe's penalty area was under almost constant siege for the remainder of the first half. Sam had little to do and he became aware of people on the touchline pointing at one goal and then the other.

The Brimthorpe teacher called out to Mr Rogers.

It's not half-time yet. What's the matter?

Hey, Ref! Stop the game!

The man strode over to the Brimthorpe goal and paced out the distance between the posts.

Sam's heart sank when he saw him start to head up the pitch in his direction.

What are you doing?

I reckon our goal is bigger than yours – and I'm going to prove it.

It can't be, surely. They are adjustable, but...

Sam tried to explain to the teachers as well.

Sam's pitiful face was enough to convince anyone he was telling the truth.

His dad rushed on to the scene, breathless and embarrassed after finding out what had happened.

Sorry. I just nipped back home to fetch my lad's goalie gloves.

Don't blame him. It's my fault, I should have double-checked the measurements.

We're not cheats. We'll award you the game, if you like.

No, it's OK. Just one of those things, I guess.

Sam spoke up again.

Dad and me will sort out the goals so they're both the same size.

It was a genuine offer from Sam, but it made the Brimthorpe teacher laugh out loud.

No way! You'll leave them exactly as they are now. We'll see how you get on guarding a bigger goal for the rest of the match.

Daniel summed up the battle that lay ahead.

None of us can afford to make any mistakes this half. They're really gonna throw everything at us, knowing our goal is bigger.

Same for both sides in the end, though, I suppose.

Not in this weather, it isn't. It's blowing a gale now – and it's starting to rain.

The captain turned to his goalkeeper.

As the second half kicked off, the wind and rain lashed into the faces of the Southfield players. Sam swallowed hard, grateful that at least he'd be able to grip the wet ball better now that he had his gloves.

Sam was called into action straightaway as a shot curled and dipped in the swirling wind. Somehow, he managed to get his hands and body behind the ball, dropping to his knees and clinging safely onto it.

The busier he became, the better Sam played. He made a whole string of good saves, including touching a powerful, close-range header onto the crossbar.

Nobody could quite believe it when Southfield broke away and snatched the lead, totally against the run of play.

The Brimthorpe keeper, cold from standing around, let a weak shot from Ajit slither through his legs and over the line.

As time began to run out for the visitors, they became more and more frantic. Their shooting was often wild, too high or wide, even with the bigger goal to aim at.

Sam dealt well with anything they managed to get on target...

...and was pleased to tip a fierce strike past the right post.

'Goal, Ref!' claimed the Brimthorpe captain loudly. 'It went just inside the post. Anybody could see that.'

To Southfield's astonishment, instead of giving a corner, Mr Rogers suddenly pointed to the centre-circle.

Daniel protested as much as he dared.

That wasn't in, Mr Rogers. Sam pushed it wide.

Boosted by the gift of an equaliser, Brimthorpe nearly went and scored the winner. In a last mad scramble in Sam's muddy penalty area, he blocked one effort from point-blank range and then Josh kicked another off the line.

The two boys grinned at each other.

Thanks for that one, Josh.

The final whistle signalled a 2–2 draw and the boys were confident they could win the replay. To no one's great surprise, Mr Rogers again named Sam as 'Man of the Match', but this time he made sure he put Sam's mind at rest first.

Sam smiled sheepishly.

Not yet, thanks, Mr Rogers. Maybe when I've got a bit better at that sort of thing.

His dad was waiting for him outside and gave him a slap on the back.

Well played, son. You showed 'em what you can do.